Our Ocean Home

by Robert Lyn Nelson

NORTHWORD PRESS
Chanhassen, Minnesota
www.northwordpress.com

NorthWord Press
18705 Lake Drive East
Chanhassen, MN 55317
1-800-328-3895
www.northwordpress.com

Designed by
Russell S. Kuepper

Library of Congress Cataloging-in-Publication Data
Nelson, Robert Lyn.
    Our ocean home / Robert Lyn Nelson.
      p. cm.
    ISBN 1-55971-596-0 (hc)
     1. Marine animals—Juvenile literature.   2. Marine ecology—Juvenile
literature. 3. Ocean—Juvenile literature. ·[1. Marine animals. 2. Ocean
3. Conservation of natural resources.]
    I. Title.
    QL122.2.N45 1997
    591.77—dc21   96-46822

Printed in Singapore

10 9 8 7 6 5

This book is for
Margaux and Sienna
and for Mason

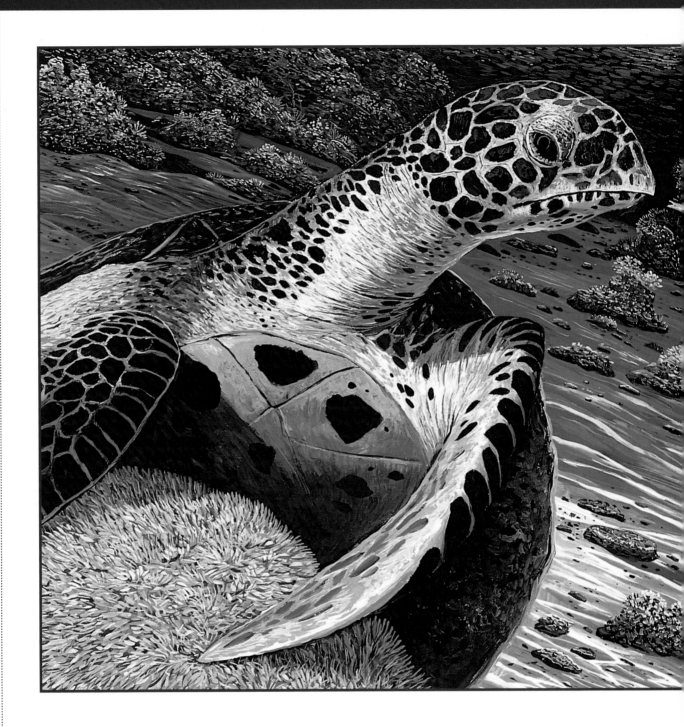

My name is Honu, the turtle. My home is in the ocean, but the ocean also belongs to you, and to all the other children around the world.

Our

ocean is a
magical
place, with
brightly
colored
butterfly
fish that
dart and
swoop and
seem to fly
through
the water.

Sometimes
the waves whisper when they wash along the beach, and sometimes they crash like thunder. Below the surface, all is quiet as small fish glide through the blue-green, glittering sea.

Mother

monk seals teach their pups how to find food, and friendly stingrays spread their wing-like fins. Many, many fishes and plants and sea creatures make their home beneath the waves and among the currents.

Gentle humpback whales spray bright fountains in the air, and dive deep into the sea with a mighty splash. They sing mysterious, enchanted songs, and it is a wonder to watch them pass.

All of us who dwell in the sea are brothers and sisters, from the very large to the very small.

 **Tiny** seahorses ride the ripples in a beautiful garden of coral on our secret ocean floor.

In the whole world there is more ocean than land, and the different oceans touch each other. A drop of water at the beach might have come from India or Australia or the island of Bora Bora.

So sea lions truly play in all the waters of the world as the seagulls and pelicans fly overhead.

I have lived a long life, but our ocean home has become smaller over the years. Some places are not as nice to live in anymore. The sea is fragile, and our ocean family needs your help to keep it clean and safe.

The spotted dolphins need sparkling water to play like joyful children, leaping in the waves. The sun reflects off their skin like hundreds of tiny rainbows.

know you will help keep a place for
everyone in our ocean. It is a place
for all, even the unusual frogfish who
changes its color to yellow or orange,
or brown or gray or red.

The

sea is home for creatures with scales or smooth skin or fur. Sea otters float on top of the water instead of living beneath the waves. The ocean must be healthy for them, too.

We all share the ocean and we depend on each other to live. We must never take more than we need. Even many, many fish can run out and become extinct, so there are never any more of them. Monk seals and sea otters, humpback whales and green sea turtles almost became extinct.

Rain

falling on the land goes back to the ocean. Streams and rivers and waterfalls flow to the sea. All my family of ocean creatures need clean, fresh water so their food will grow, and they won't become sick, and new babies will be born.

The beautiful ocean is often quiet. Starfish and striped shells rest on the sand.

Each day begins with sunrise glowing golden on the sea. Fish swim peacefully through the water. At night the moon will turn the waves to silver.

As the day ends with sunset, our ocean family searches for food. The sky and clouds turn red and gold, pink and purple, and deepest shades of blue.

Our ocean home is powerful and exciting. It was here before there was land, and before people. It has always been here for us.

We all share this world, the ocean creatures and you. We are family. Some day, when you and your friends grow up, the ocean will belong to your children too.